Leadership Curriculum for Music Students

For band, orchestra, and choir

SCOTT LANG

Alfred Music
P.O. Box 10003
Van Nuys, CA 91410-0003
alfred.com

ISBN-10: 1-4706-4196-8
ISBN-13: 978-1-4706-4196-2

I'm excited that you're here!

This book is designed to help facilitate a collaborative process between both student leaders and program directors. While each can use these materials individually, I recommend using this workbook in a collaborative group setting to unlock its full potential. Some activities are geared more toward the individual, some focus on the group as a whole, and others are a perfect marriage between the two. Regardless of the structure, each unit and activity is designed to benefit everyone involved in the process.

Drawing upon thirty years of experience in the classroom and as a leadership facilitator, I believe that all great leadership-training experiences have a few things in common:

- They allow you to be **creative**.
- They are **adaptable** and fit your unique situation.
- They are **engaging** and **interactive**.
- And most importantly, they **focus on you**.

Thoughts to keep in mind as you progress

THE HEART OF LEADERSHIP IS NOT IN WHAT WE KNOW, BUT THE CHOICES WE MAKE

Because of this, you will find far more questions in this book than you will answers. My goal for this workbook is based less in teaching concepts than it is asking you the right questions—so you can have your own "Aha!" moments throughout.

LEADERSHIP TRAINING IS A JOURNEY, NOT A DESTINATION

That's why this workbook was designed to be highly interactive. As with anything else in life, the more you are willing to put into the experience, the more you will get out of it. Knowing this, I hope that you will take time to process and reflect, and use this as a vehicle for self-discovery and personal growth.

THIS BOOK IS NOT MEANT TO BE HOMEWORK!

Take your time. Invest in the experience. After all, it means you're investing in yourself! In answering the questions, remember that your thoughts have intrinsic value just as they are. Don't try to impress anyone with "the right answer." You are a unique person with unique perspectives, and your thoughts and beliefs as a leader should be reflected in these activities.

As a part of this book, you will also find tools to aid in the leadership selection process. Your director may use these tools as is or alter them for your group. Either way, the bottom line is the same: to build a leadership team that reflects the needs of your music ensemble.

Enjoy the workbook, and good luck on your leadership journey!

UNIT 1
YOURSELF

"IT IS HARD TO FAIL,

BUT IT IS WORSE

NEVER TO HAVE TRIED TO SUCCEED."

—Theodore Roosevelt

1 DEFINING LEADERSHIP THROUGH YOUR LENS

Within the past hundred years, there have been enough books written on what we *think about* leadership to fill entire libraries. Despite this, what we *know about* leadership would easily fit into a small bookshelf. In this chapter, we will begin to explore some commonly held leadership beliefs and see how these beliefs match up with *your* personal ideologies.

I wish there were a simple answer to the question, "What is leadership?" The truth is, there isn't a straightforward way to explain it. I wish there were a unified rubric and set of character traits that could apply to all countries, cultures, and people. But it's a highly complex and individual concept. Needless to say, I think I'll be wishing for a while longer.

Leadership is situational and personal.

Often, leadership looks very different depending on the person and the context. For instance, a freshman who is late on the first day of school because they don't know where the rehearsal room is wouldn't be treated the same as a senior who is late for the fifth time this week. A student who didn't practice last night because of a family emergency wouldn't be treated the same as the student who never bothered to take their instrument home. A student who is struggling to memorize an excerpt is thought of very differently than a student who might be struggling with depression.

The point is, every person is unique. Every situation is unique. Every leader is unique. To my way of thinking, there are as many ways to lead as there are people to be led. This is precisely why leadership is more of an art than a science. That said, there are a few guiding questions that I always return to:

- Am I doing what I think is right?
- Am I doing what I think is right for the person I am leading?
- Am I doing it in service of that person?

There are no formulas for leadership. Every situation and person is different. Always do what you think is right, in the situation you are in and for the person you are dealing with.

This chapter and the following questions are designed to help you get to the essence of what you believe about student leadership, and how it applies to your group. Keep in mind, as you grow and evolve, and as your group changes, so will your beliefs. Student leadership, like everything else in life, is a dynamic and ever-evolving pursuit. As you grow and change, so will your beliefs. While it is important to have conviction in your beliefs, it is equally important to not become mired in them like quicksand.

Reflect on the following questions to discover what your views on leadership are. Feel free to revisit your answers throughout the year and see how your beliefs change and evolve.

QUESTIONS

What is student leadership to you?

What qualities does an effective student leader possess?

In the past year, how have you succeeded in displaying those qualities? How have you failed?

List at least five behaviors that student leaders exhibit in your group:

What things should a leader in your group do to help students who are struggling? You can reference real-life examples from your group without naming names:

How much of a leader were you in the past six months?

1 **2** **3** **4** **5**

NOT A LEADER AT ALL — VERY MUCH A LEADER

Justify your answer:

If someone were to ask the members of your section what kind of leader they think you are, what do you think they might say? List three positive things that might be said:

____

____

____

List three negative things that might be said:

____

____

____

Do you think that you treat everyone in your group the same, regardless of year, instrument, musical talent, or other factors? ______

Explain your answer: ______________________________

____

____

What are some areas of self-improvement that you can identify in how you treat the members of your group?

____

____

____

Describe one situation within your group that you are proud of how you handled:

____

____

____

Describe one situation within your group that you could have handled better:

____

____

____

"JUST BECAUSE YOU HAVEN'T

FOUND YOUR TALENT YET,

DOESN'T MEAN YOU DON'T HAVE ONE."

—*Kermit the Frog*

2 YOUR BLESSINGS AND CURSES

Without going into great detail, suffice it to say that I believe that the person you are is, by and large, the person you will likely always be. Yes, you will grow. Yes, you will experience many things. Yes, you will become more seasoned and educated. But will you fundamentally change as a person? Probably not.

As people, leaders, musicians, and students, we all have "strengths and weaknesses." But there is something about that term that doesn't convey the inner parts of us that are fixed or unchanging. So instead, I like to think of strengths and weaknesses as blessings and curses. For example:

- **I am more patient now than when I was 16, but I am still impatient by nature.**
- **I am more empathetic now than when I was 16, but I am still not empathetic by nature.**
- **I am a better listener now than I was when I was 16, but I am still not a good listener by nature.**
- **I am more focused now, but I am still easily distracted by nature.**

These are my "curses." We all have them. That is part of being human. But we all have "blessings" as well. For example:

- **I was always good at talking in front of people, but I am better now.**
- **I was always comfortable teaching, but I am better now.**
- **I was always effective at managing conflict, but I am better now.**
- **I was always a creative problem solver, but I am better now.**

Key Takeaway

Too often we try to mold ourselves to fit a job or situation—when the better and easier pathway might be to step up to roles that let you lead and serve with your natural talents.

I believe that a key component to being a successful leader is understanding and acknowledging your true self; the good, the bad, and the ugly, and placing yourself in a position where you can do the most good for the most amount of people.

In short, you do the most good when you are doing what you are most good at.

It's important not to spend time and effort trying to be something you're not, but rather, spending that same time and effort leveraging what you are naturally good at. Using myself as an example, here are some things I am naturally good at:

- **I am better in front of groups than in individual conversations.**
- **I am more comfortable in dealing with behaviors than feelings.**
- **I am a better talker than listener.**
- **I am better with big ideas than small details.**
- **I am a morning person and tend to lose focus towards the end of the day.**

Knowing and accepting these things about myself, I am able to better position myself in roles and responsibilities that will best serve the others and the group. If I place myself in areas that require skills that I lack, I am not only setting up my group for failure, but also making myself miserable in the process.

In other words, take stock of yourself and find your **leadership fit**.

Disclaimer: This concept is not an excuse to avoid or refuse to do things that you are not good at (Example: I'm not good at practicing, so I shouldn't practice). For this example, it means that you are honest enough with yourself to pursue a leadership role that is not <u>dependent</u> on your being the best player in the section, but perhaps something else.

Now it's time to get to know you!

QUESTIONS

List three blessings you have:

List three curses you have:

List a current job in the group that most closely aligns with your <u>blessings</u> and explain why:

List a current job in the group that most closely aligns with your <u>curses</u> and explain why:

What are some tasks below that would feature your blessings? Circle the ones that you think you could assist with:

teaching music	fundraising	locker check in/out	warm-ups	stretches
equipment repair	daily announcements	equipment inventory	purchase orders	tuning
taking attendance	teaching drill	uniform inventory	posters	organizing
setting up equipment	website/social media	music memory checks	concert setup	music library
field maintenance	running meetings	bulletin board	concert programs	cleaning
uniform handout	music stand repair	rehearsal set up	creating fun activities	recording
celebrating birthdays	bus requests	making copies	phone tree	decorating

Now list five things *not listed above* that could be of service to the organization:

____

____

Knowing what you know about the organization and yourself, create a new job that best suits your blessings and curses. The job should offer real value to the group and have concrete responsibilities:

Job title: ______________________________

Job description: ______________________________

____

Daily responsibilities: ______________________________

____

Weekly responsibilities: ______________________________

____

____

How would this job differ from the ones already existing within the organization?

____

____

What are three ways this job will have an impact on the group or an individual within the group?

____

____

Why should you be chosen for this job?

____

____

"A GOOD LEADER TAKES A LITTLE MORE

THAN HIS SHARE OF THE BLAME,

A LITTLE LESS THAN HIS SHARE OF THE CREDIT."

—Arnold H. Glasow

3 LEADERSHIP BY EXAMPLE

Now that we have an understanding of your "blessings and curses" it's time to see how they have impacted your choices and actions in the past. This can be an uncomfortable but important process as we look to the mirror and see if you are the person others want you to be—or more importantly, if you are the person that you want to be.

ARE YOU A GOOD ROLE MODEL?

From the moment we are born, we learn by watching. We learned to walk, talk, eat, and play by watching others and modeling their behavior.

Educationally speaking, it is the most efficient and expedient way to teach someone something.

Musically speaking, the same holds true. Would you rather have an articulation described for you to figure it out—or played for you to model after? Would you rather read and assimilate a chapter on good marching technique, or have someone show you how to march? Would you rather have someone to explain how to assemble/maintain/clean your instrument, or show you how to do it?

The same holds true for leadership. Followers often mimic the behaviors of their leaders. In my experience working with all kinds of groups, I can say these statements with confidence:

- Show me a lazy section; chances are they are led by a lazy leader
- Show me a section that does not practice; chances are they are led by someone who does not practice
- Show me a disrespectful section; chances are they are led by a disrespectful leader
- Show me a mean section; chances are they are led by a mean leader

Role modeling is a quick, efficient, and powerful way that leaders influence the groups that they lead. In the end, your followers likely represent your best and worst characteristics. What you see in them is often what they see in you.

ASKING THE HARD QUESTIONS

Are you someone who leads by example? Are you someone who sets the standard for others to follow? Are you someone that others actually want to follow? Are you someone who models the highest ideals and behaviors?

Honest self-assessment is one of the hardest things to do. Sometimes, we overlook our own shortcomings while being all too quick to spot them in others. Other times, we are far too critical of ourselves as we give others the benefit of the doubt. In this unit, you will be challenged to take a long, hard look in the mirror and see if you are modeling the very beliefs you claimed to espouse in the previous unit. Leading by example is a key component to being a true leader, and before we can look forward, it is important that we first look back on our past actions.

If you are being honest with yourself, this may be the hardest chapter of all.

It is important that you try to be as objective as possible and see yourself as others see you. You need not be overly critical, nor should you gloss over some areas of possible self-improvement. Every journey of self-improvement begins with self-assessment.

The questions that follow are designed to assist you with the self-reflection process. Your answers may make you uncomfortable, but if dealt with honestly, will make you a better leader. Ask yourself this: Would I rather fail with style or lead with flaws?

And with that, we end this chapter with the same question we began it with:

Are you a good role model?

QUESTIONS

List up to three behaviors you exhibit that you would want your section to model:

List up to three behaviors you exhibit that you would not want your section to model:

Circle the appropriate answer:

Do you ask others to practice their music and not always do it yourself?	YES	NO	SOMETIMES
Do you ask others to work hard and not always do it yourself?	YES	NO	SOMETIMES
Do you ask others to be respectful and not always do it yourself?	YES	NO	SOMETIMES
Do you ask others to show up on time and not always do it yourself?	YES	NO	SOMETIMES
Do you ask for dedication and not always demonstrate it yourself?	YES	NO	SOMETIMES
Do you expect your peers to support your director's decision but not always do it yourself?	YES	NO	SOMETIMES

What else do you ask of others that you are not always doing yourself? Be honest!

In what ways do your peers mimic your behaviors within the group?

List three good ways:

List three bad ways:

List five words you think your peers would use to describe you:

List five words you think your teacher would use to describe you:

List three things you plan on changing next year when it comes to being a better role model. Be specific and honest:

"BE YOURSELF;

EVERYONE ELSE IS TAKEN."

— *Oscar Wilde*

4 BEING YOURSELF

Before we move on to your team, I just wanted to share a couple of final thoughts on being "you."

Finding one's own personal pathway is the ultimate challenge and primary purpose of the teenage experience. Other than your first two years as an infant, there is no period of your life in which your mind and body will experience such a radical, personal, physical, and intellectual transformation. Think about the transformation your mind, body, and spirit will go through during the forty-five months you will spend as a member of your high school group. For some, the change will leave them almost unrecognizable in every way.

It's so hard to "be yourself" when "yourself" is changing almost daily. Add to that the pressure of the human fishbowl that is high school, and it's not hard to understand why BEING a teenager is so difficult. When you add the responsibility of LEADING teenagers when you are one yourself, it becomes overwhelming at times. All you can do is "be yourself" and "trust your instincts."

THE AUTHENTICITY BUZZ

"Authentic" is one of the new buzzwords in the leadership movement Bookshelves at retail stores are crammed with books that claim to help you find your authentic self. The books claim to help you look inside yourself and see the true you for who you are. Isn't it ironic that we look to someone else to help us find something only we can see? In the end, this new leadership movement of authenticity is really just a trendy way of saying three things:

1. *Lead from your strengths.* Do what you do best, admit what you don't do well, focus on those things that you are exceptional at, and ask for help in the areas where you are not.
2. *Don't be a poser.* No one wants to follow a fake, so be honest about who you are, both with yourself and with others. Know what you believe and act on those beliefs consistently, regardless of who you are with and where you are.
3. *Don't do what has already been done.* You were chosen for a reason. You are an individual unlike any other, with talents unlike any other, so use them unlike any other. Think "outside of the box" and bring some new, fresh ideas to the position and your role as a leader.

Of course, there is nothing wrong with doing what's been done before, but use this as an opportunity to put your personal stamp on a past process by giving it an update or new spin to reflect your style of leadership. After all, if the only thing that changed from last year was the person in charge, we probably don't need the person in charge.

Key Takeaway

As a teenager, being authentic is hard because you are still developing who you are. True authenticity starts with vulnerability. Take a chance every once in a while and be honest with yourself and your friends about what you REALLY believe, think, and feel.

UNIT 2
YOUR TEAM

“BE A YARDSTICK OF QUALITY.

SOME PEOPLE AREN’T USED TO

AN ENVIRONMENT WHERE

EXCELLENCE IS EXPECTED.”

—*Steve Jobs*

5 LEADERSHIP TEAM ASSESSMENT

Prior to preparing any future plan, it is important to know your starting point so you can measure your growth. As a part of this process, it's also important to note what is working really well and needs to be left alone.

Take some time to consider the questions and answer them thoroughly and honestly. This is not a gripe session, just a chance to know your group's strengths and weaknesses. Try to set aside situations involving individuals and focus on the group as a whole.

To read and complete this section of the course will take some time (approximately 30–45 minutes) so be sure you have the time to complete it before starting.

Key Takeaway

These assessments and the subsequent discussion of them should give you a good idea about your starting point, both as a program and as its leadership team. As you process all of the answers, focus on coming to a consensus on where you are currently and where you would like to be when the process is done. In other words, you are striving for a common point of origination and a destination. When these two things have been discussed fully, you will be well on your way toward being a more effective leadership team.

QUESTIONS

Rate the following statement: Our leadership team is cohesive and active.

1 2 3 4 5

STRONGLY DISAGREE — STRONGLY AGREE

Our previous leadership team's strengths were:

____

____

Our previous leadership team's weaknesses were:

____

____

In the past, the people on the leadership team have been people who displayed the following trait(s) (circle all that apply):

dedication	compassion	care	commitment	initiative
character	vision	risk-taking	ownership	cynicism
sarcasm	anger	patience	laziness	power
hunger/drive	shyness	humor	meanness	honesty
productivity	a strong work ethic			

Our goals for this year as a group are clear and measurable? YES NO MAYBE

Our leadership hierarchy is clear? YES NO MAYBE

List the top three strengths of your music program:

List the top three weaknesses of your music program:

If we had to characterize our program's strengths as a whole, the following words would best describe it (circle all that apply):

performance	character	innovation	excellence	mediocrity
care	charity	personality	school spirit	friendliness
musicality	humor	politeness	respect	pride
integrity	auxiliary	jazz	dedication	competitiveness

List any other words not found in the above:

If we had to characterize our program's weaknesses as a whole, the following words would best describe them (circle all that apply):

performance	character	innovation	excellence	mediocrity
care	charity	personality	school spirit	friendliness
musicality	humor	politeness	respect	pride
integrity	auxiliary	jazz	dedication	competitiveness

List any other words not found in the above word groupings:

In the space provided, answer the following questions. Whenever possible, please make all answers as specific and measurable as possible. For instance, where it asks for your greatest hope, instead of writing, "For everyone to be more dedicated," write this instead: "For our perfect attendance awards to increase by 10%" or "For our small group meetings to increase to every week instead of every other week." The more measurable and specific your destination, the more likely you are to know it when you see it.

How often does the leadership team currently meet?

Is it sufficient? If not, why?

Rate the following statement: My job description matches my strengths and limits my weaknesses.

1 2 3 4 5

STRONGLY DISAGREE STRONGLY AGREE

My greatest hope for this year:

My greatest fear for this year:

The general culture of the group is:

AMAZING THRIVING HEALTHY ADEQUATE NEGATIVE UNHEALTHY TOXIC

No matter what, we need to accomplish the following three things:

I would classify this year as successful if:

I would classify this year as a failure if:

Other thoughts I would like to discuss:

“NEVER DOUBT THAT A SMALL GROUP
OF THOUGHTFUL, CONCERNED CITIZENS
CAN CHANGE THE WORLD.
INDEED IT IS THE ONLY THING THAT EVER HAS.”

—Margaret Mead

6 GOAL SETTING

Setting and achieving goals is an important part of any leadership journey. Even in failure, the desire to strive for something difficult to attain is a noble act in and of itself. Setting and attaining goals is where your leadership journey takes on a life of its own. Now is the time when you are no longer training to be a leader but are expected to act like a leader. Everything up to this point will prove to be pointless if you are unable or unwilling to take the next step: TO ACTUALLY LEAD, execute, and help move the group toward its desired goals!

A good, honest place to start is to think about all of the goals you have set in the past that you have failed to achieve, and you'll get a sense for what lies ahead. Remember your last New Year's resolution? Remember the goal you set on the first day of school last year to procrastinate less and work harder? Remember all of the things you said you were going to do during your summer vacation?

I think you get the idea that most people don't even remember, much less achieve, their goals.

Goals without action are called wishes.

There is nothing wrong with wishing for something, hoping that it will magically appear, as long as everyone understands it is a wish. The problem occurs when others are counting on you and your leadership peers to help the group achieve them, only to find that they were more wishes than goals.

THE THREE PITFALLS OF GOAL-SETTING

Believe it or not, most people fail to achieve their goals, not because they are unwilling participants, but because they were doomed to fail from the start. Most goals go unrealized because of three missteps:

1. The leaders were unwilling to do the work required for success.
2. The leaders set faulty, unrealistic goals to begin with.
3. The leaders had no specific plan of action to achieve their goals.

Goals are nothing more than destinations on a map. It's something to point to and dream about how awesome it would be to get there. The key is in the planning of the trip.

For further clarification and understanding, let's take a quick look at each of the three pitfalls. Review these materials before and after you have set your goals to ensure that you have not set yourself up for failure.

1. *Unwillingness to do the work.* Let's be blunt: There is nothing anyone can do about this but YOU. You and you alone have to commit to doing what is required to get the job done. This is where the vision ends and accountability begins. There will be others who will help and support you, but this does not mean they will do the work for you. At times, it will be important that you don't walk alone as a leader. Your student leader colleagues will walk with you, but don't expect them to carry you.

2. *Faulty goal-setting.* Most goals are doomed from the start as they are unattainable or unreasonable to begin with. Failure is oftentimes inevitable when the goal lacks specificity, is too large, or is not within the goal setter's sphere of control.

   Example: **Our goal is to be the best group in the state.**

   While this goal sounds great, the leap it would take to achieve that in one year is often unrealistic, and unless your state has a way of measuring who is the "best group," then there is no way of knowing whether or not you have achieved it.

   Additionally, there are many elements needed to achieve the example goal which are not under your sphere of control. This includes staff hiring, show design, music selection, enrollment, budget, scheduling, etc. When in doubt, it is best to set goals in very small increments and under very tight time parameters.

   Here's what the example goal would look like, revised:

   Our goal is to raise our music score, visual score, and auxiliary score by 10% from our scores last year at the same event.

   This is a more concrete and realistic way of not only approaching the goal, but also knowing whether or not it has been achieved through a metric.

3. *No specific plan of action.* All goals require an actionable roadmap, and all action plans require three things: specificity, timetables, and ways to measure success on the way to the goal. Without these three elements, you are more likely to wallow in ambiguity and frustration.

   Example: **Our goal is for our section to be the best section in the group.**

   While this is a noble goal, it lacks the three requirements for a good plan of action. Based on this example, it lacks a timetable, specifics on what constitutes the best section, and how the group will know if it has achieved the goal. A better way of phrasing this goal might be:

   Our goal is to be the first section in our group camp to correctly memorize the entire opener and pass our playing test with a 90% proficiency or higher. To achieve this, we will meet every day during our lunch break for fifteen minutes until everyone passes the playing test. If, after three days, not every one has passed the test, we will assign each person who has not passed it a "playing buddy" who will give them private lessons on the music until they pass.

Key Takeaway

Break everything down into small pieces (hour by hour, day by day) and it will make the journey more rewarding and enjoyable.

This is just one example of making your goals and their implementation more concrete and attainable. Once you have established goals that are realistic and an action plan to back it up, the only thing standing between you and success is YOU (see pitfall #1).

Like everything else in life, the more you practice something, the better you will be at it. With that in mind, use the space below to list three goals for your section or group. When you are done, share your goals with someone else from the leadership team (or the entire team) and get their feedback on how you can improve its structure/process for success. When picking your goals, it might be wise to consider one musical goal, one behavioral goal, and one team-building goal. This will give you a broad base of success from which to build upon for future goal-setting activities.

Pick three goals you would like the leadership team to consider for the upcoming year:

Goal #1

Timeline: ____________________

Specific actions required for success: ____________________

____

People responsible: ____________________

____

Notes: ____________________

____

____

Goal #2

Timeline: ____________________

Specific actions required for success: ____________________

____

People responsible: ____________________

____

Notes: ____________________

____

____

Goal #3

Timeline: ____________________

Specific actions required for success: ____________________

____

People responsible: ____________________

____

Notes: ____________________

____

____

"YOU CAN DISAGREE

WITHOUT BEING DISAGREEABLE."

—*Ruth Bader Ginsberg*

7 GETTING ALONG

In this chapter, we will talk about how to deal with the different types of people you might encounter as a part of your leadership role. We can't all be best friends, but we can all get along!

The ability to get along with others on the leadership team is an important prerequisite for leadership and for life. This is not to say that all leaders have to be gregarious and outgoing people who enjoy being in the presence of others—but that they are secure enough in their role and views to be comfortable with different opinions and leadership styles.

Power struggles are not uncommon among leadership teams. Grounded in ego and fear, people seek to place themselves in dominant roles to the benefit of themselves and the detriment of others. This "me" mentality is as destructive of a disease as any that can afflict a group. Your peers are often caught up in the pettiness and choose sides, escalating and widening the conflict. Just remember, **your value comes not from your strength but from your service!**

INTROVERTS AND EXTROVERTS

History is full of many powerful and influential leaders who were introverts, shying away from the attention that came with their positions. They measured their worth by the work they were able to do and the people they were able to help rather than the attention they were able to garner. History looks kindly on those who forsake the spotlight in the name of good deeds.

Although it is impossible to love every person all of the time, know that the more your peers like and trust you, the more they will want to be led by you. Also, the more your director likes and trusts you, the more they will let you lead. Be likable and trustable in the face of conflict!

But some jobs come with the spotlight, which makes them more or less attractive to certain leaders. For some, the spotlight of leadership is easier to deal with. Keep in mind that some jobs require fewer people skills and less interaction than others. That is not to say that you can lead through email or text, but it is important to know if your responsibilities as a leader match your persona.

For example, jobs such as a music librarian or group webmaster require less student interaction than jobs like a drum major or section leader. Concertmaster could very well be an introvert, speaking through their music, while the morale officer is the life of the party. While managing both tasks and relationships is key to being an effective leader, some jobs require less management than others.

There will be disagreements.

The ability to get along is an important part of being an effective leader and leadership team. After all, it is people that you are leading (yes, drummers count as people). This does not mean that each and every member of the leadership team must be your best friend, but that **your relationship does not impede your ability to effectively lead.**

As a part of your leadership role, you might have a conflict with another leader or someone who is difficult to deal with. What's critical is that you resolve it amongst yourselves and not involve others. When you fight fire with fire, the fire only gets bigger. Whether this is done with intent or out of ignorance, the fact remains the same: You only hurt yourself when you hurt others. As unreasonable as it may seem, some people thrive on trauma and drama. A leader shouldn't be one of those people.

MORE THAN YOUR PEERS

Beyond your relationships with your peers, there is the personal dynamic between the director and the leaders to consider as well. The same understanding of conflict resolution applies here and is even more important. If you and your director are unable to function as a team and to see eye-to-eye on what is best for the group, then regardless of your ability to get along with your peers, you are doomed to fail.

This director/student relationship, more than any other, is based on trust. Your director has placed a group of young people in your trust. For you to respond in any manner that jeopardizes that trust should cause everyone to examine your readiness to effectively lead and be led. A student leader with a good relationship with his/her peers—and a bad relationship with his/her director—is like a car with a big engine and no brakes: destined for a crash.

QUESTIONS

Would you say that you are a flexible person who "rolls with the punches"?

What are your "hot-button" issues/pet peeves that cause you to feel more uncompromising as a leader? (Inefficiency with time, disrespect, poor work ethic, etc.)

Would you consider yourself to be a loyal person?

Is there someone on the leadership team that you already have a conflict with? If so, how do you plan on dealing with it?

Describe your relationship with your director in three words:

Have you ever questioned the director behind their back? YES NO

Have you ever made yourself look good at the expense of someone else on the team? If so, describe what happened (without using names):

List three things you think the leadership team can do to be more cohesive moving forward:

Write a practice note below

If appropriate, feel free to apologize to someone you have wronged in the past so you can move forward. "I'm sorry" are two of the most powerful words you can say to another person.

"LIFE IS A SERIES OF NATURAL

AND SPONTANEOUS CHANGES.

DON'T RESIST THEM; THAT ONLY CREATES SORROW.

LET REALITY BE REALITY.

LET THINGS FLOW NATURALLY FORWARD

IN WHATEVER WAY THEY LIKE."

—*Lao Tzu*

8 EMBRACING CHANGE

This chapter deals head-on with the issue of change. Nobody likes change, but it is a critical part of ensuring that your group continues to move forward productively.

If you know me, then you know that I am a creature of habit. I am no more qualified to offer advice on change than I am on how to be an NBA power forward. I take comfort in knowing that my surroundings are of my own making and are just as I left them. I order the same thing time and time again when I visit my favorite restaurants. I buy the same tennis shoes over and over, and believe it or not, I wore the same type of clothing to rehearsal so often (khaki shorts and white t-shirt) that one Halloween, my entire band showed up dressed like me. I am not what anyone would describe as a "change agent."

For me, change brings about fear of the unknown, fear of failure, and a general sense of being uncomfortable. It is hard knowing that what brought you success in the past will not necessarily bring similar results in the future. Despite my emotional attachment to yesteryear, my intellect knows that if I repeat the same behaviors as last year, not only will my score not be the same, but it will more than likely yield less positive results. This means that whenever possible, I try to make sure that my intellect overrides my instinct, and I find myself moving forward, despite feeling a bit wobbly or insecure.

There are few activities that are changing at the speed of music. What was cutting-edge five years ago is dated now. There is no other subject in school that necessitates adaptability the way music does. Those groups that consistently resist change (or manage it poorly) will find themselves falling behind quicker than they might think.

Music groups are different than other groups.

If you are like me, chances are that you find comfort in repetition. Music groups use repetition as a teaching tool more than any other curricular area. But ironically, no other area in the public school system has seen the changes in skill, team camaraderie, and personal development as your group has. To that point, change is not only good, but required for success.

There are very few activities and subjects in high school that endure the level of change that music groups do. Think about it: How much have Shakespeare's sonnets, the Pythagorean Theorem, or Newton's Laws changed in the past three hundred years?

If the class of 2018 masters the chapter on Newton's Laws, do they make the law harder for the class of 2019? The answer is NO! The curriculum is neither fluid nor dynamic and does nothing to meet the needs of students as their skillsets grow and evolve.

Whether it's new uniforms, drill, choreography, instruments, or music, what was successful in the past will not yield success in the future. Music education doesn't just thrive on change—it demands it.

As uncomfortable as it can be, **highly successful groups understand that change is the singular constant required for success**. I am not suggesting that change for change's sake is what we are after, but that meaningful and well thought-out change will help your group reach the next level.

Now, let's take a look at change as it relates to your group. If you are in a group that is in the midst of a director change, you will want to pay particularly close attention to this unit.

QUESTIONS

List three things that you would not want to change about your program:

List three things that you would like to see changed about your program:

Rate the following statements:

I trust my director.					**My director can trust me.**				
1	**2**	**3**	**4**	**5**	**1**	**2**	**3**	**4**	**5**
STRONGLY DISAGREE				STRONGLY AGREE	STRONGLY DISAGREE				STRONGLY AGREE

What are some things you could do to improve the above numbers (if applicable)?

What is your group's perception of the leadership team?

How can you improve that (if applicable)?

UNIT 3

YOUR JOB

"LEADERS THINK AND TALK

ABOUT THE SOLUTIONS.

FOLLOWERS THINK AND TALK

ABOUT THE PROBLEMS."

— *Brian Tracy*

9 TAKING INITIATIVE

Taking initiative is REALLY hard in music groups.

As music students, we are trained to do nothing until we are told to do something. Literally, we take even the most basic functions that others take for granted and turn them into an exercise of compliance; when to sit, when to stand, when to put our instruments up, when to play, and even when to breathe. We have a culture within music that says, "Wait to do something until you are told."

About the only choice you get to make is the color of your underwear, unless of course you have white uniform pants, then we even help you with that! Music creates great followers, which can result in very confused leaders.

MILITARY ROOTS

Part of this culture is rooted in survival—after all, you can't have a hundred students in a class doing whatever they want. But a militaristic background underpins the activity (Fun fact: marching band actually *started* in the military). The activity prides itself on uniformity—the ability to do things not just the same way, but to do them together. The better the uniformity, the better the ensemble. Yes, uniformity and conformity are essential to a successful music student—but not a successful music leader. This is where you must dig in.

What made you successful as a follower will not make you successful as a leader. As a follower, err on the side of silence and compliance—but as a leader, always try to err on the side of action and accountability.

THE BALANCING ACT

To be a good music student, you need to do what you're told, how you're told, and when you're told. To be a good leader, you have to do things when you're not told, how you think they need to be done, and when they need to be done.

One is the role of a follower; the other is the role of the leader.

One role is concrete and concise; the other is vague and lacks clarity.

One role has a start and end date; the other is a continuing journey.

One role has implications for the individual; the other has a bigger impact on the ensemble's success as a whole.

But as a leader, you actually have to play *both* roles. The challenge is knowing when to be a leader and when to be a follower. For instance, have you ever found yourself in the following situations?

- You heard a wrong note, but were unsure if you should say something.
- You saw a wrong drill spot, but were unsure if you should move to fix it.
- You observed an inappropriate behavior, but were unsure if it was your place to address it.

THE SIDE OF LEADERSHIP

There is no manual or handbook to know when to lead and when to follow, but if you need to err on one side, I would encourage you to **err on the side of leadership**. Yes, this is the more uncomfortable of the two choices, but it is also the most impactful.

Knowing when to "step up" and when to "step away" is rarely an easy decision. The reason most students choose inaction over action is what we covered in the intro of this chapter: Music culture has trained the leadership right out of you.

Finding a balance between knowing when to lead and when to follow is a struggle for most student leaders. The following questions are designed to help leaders and directors explore this important issue and come to a consensus.

QUESTIONS

On a scale of 1–5 , how comfortable are you as a leader taking risks in front of the group?

1 2 3 4 5

NOT COMFORTABLE AT ALL VERY COMFORTABLE

Why?

Is initiative encouraged or discouraged in your group? How so?

Is your director a "controlling" person when it comes to the group? Cite some specific examples (be nice!):

Describe a situation in the past in which you acted as a follower instead of a leader:

Do you wish you had handled the situation differently? Explain why:

Name three distinct situations in which you should act as a follower and three distinct situations where you should act as a leader:

Time to lead:

Time to follow:

"IT IS ABSURD THAT A MAN

SHOULD RULE OTHERS,

WHO CANNOT RULE HIMSELF."

—Latin Proverb

10 DEFINING ROLES AND RESPONSIBILITIES

As a student musician, it's likely that your days are filed with the "known." You arrive at the same time every day, sit in the same place, play the same music, etc. Most people take comfort and enjoy the routine.

THE THREE C'S

In the same way, people need and appreciate **consistency**, **clarity**, and **concreteness** in a leader.

Consistency: People thrive best when they are under the stewardship of a consistent and dependable leader. Someone who is as dependable as they are predictable. This way, your fellow students know what type of person they are dealing with and what the expectations are. Are you someone who is happy one minute and mad the next? Do you have a volcanic leadership style that leaves your followers wondering which one of your many sides they will be dealing with today? If so, this may be an opportunity for personal and professional growth.

Clarity: People like clear and transparent leaders, ones who communicate what the expectations are and engage in them without making special exceptions for friends or talented people. They want to know that the rules and expectations are not only clear, but are also equally applied to all members of the ensemble. If you are someone who looks the other way when your friends transgress the rules or treat different constituencies (age/instrument/relationships) differently, this will make expectations unclear and create issues for you down the road.

Key Takeaway

You would not expect a painter to bake you a cake. Nor would you want a coach to conduct your music ensemble (although it would be very entertaining). The clearer you can define your roles, the more successful you are likely to be.

Concreteness: Regardless of your position, you are still a person. You may be a section leader, but you still are a marcher. You may be the drum major, but you still have to play your instrument in class. You may be the band president, but you are still someone's friend. Knowing when to be a friend and when to be a leader is as hard as it gets. Try to create **concrete boundaries** to help others and yourself better understand which hat you are wearing (leader/follower/friend) and when. Try using time and location as guiding points. For instance, when on the field (location) or in rehearsal (time), you are a leader and not a friend. When outside of those situations, you are a friend and not a leader.

The "unknown" is one of the scariest parts of being a leader. What will happen? How should I respond? Who will thrive and who will struggle? How will I be perceived? Will I be successful?

Since we just talked about roles and responsibilities, now is the perfect time to define them. The following questions will provide you and your section with better consistency, clarity, and concreteness. Complete the following questions, tear the page out of this book, and place it somewhere that you will see it every day.

QUESTIONS

What are three things that you should do *every day* as a leader?

What are three things that you should do *every week* as a leader?

What are three things that you should do *every month* as a leader?

What is something a previous leader did in the group that you would like to continue doing?

What is something a previous leader did in the group that you would like to change?

What are three adjectives that best describe your leadership style?

What is something a previous leader did in the group that you would like to change?

11 MOTIVATING OTHERS

Spoiler alert: There is no way that you can motivate another human being to do something they do not want to do. You can only create an environment where motivated people are drawn to be a part of your group.

Keep the functions of a magnet in mind as you reflect on this concept. As a leader, you act as a magnet. As a general rule, people seek to spend time with people who share their values, interests, and ideas. We tend to draw in closer and hold in high esteem those who we can identify with on a personal and academic level. The closer our beliefs align, the closer the relationship will be.

Think about it: Student council kids tend to hang out with student council kids. Dropouts tend to hang out with other dropouts. Smokers tend to hang out with other smokers. Gamers hang out with other gamers. And music kids hang out with...well, I think you know the answer to that one!

We use magnets to keep our purses closed, hold trains to their tracks, keep paper clips organized, and ensure our most cherished pieces of art stay stuck to the fridge. The uses for the magnet are many and mighty.

Remember, magnets also have the ability to repel with equal strength as they attract. It's important to remember that your ideals, values, and behaviors can attract some people to you and repel others from wanting to follow you.

As a leader, you are a people magnet. You have the power to both attract and repel certain types of people. What types of people do you attract and repel? Different groups (band, choir, orchestra) attract different types of members. As a leader, your section is a reflection of you. Your section members, to an extent, are a reflection of you. And remember: Your values serve not only to attract those who share your views, but to repel those people who do not.

Key Takeaway

You can't motivate someone to do something or be someone they don't want to be. All you can do is create an environment that rewards people for the behaviors you want to see.

Your magnet is your greatest asset.

It is important for you to have a clear and concise understanding of what you believe and what the group is about. This is not an area where you want to be ambivalent or unfocused. Think about it this way: What are you trying to teach, who are you trying to teach it to, and how are you going to teach it? Brevity and clarity are key to being able to communicate to everyone involved with the program. The clearer you can be about what you are trying to attract as an academic, musician, and person, the stronger your bond will be with those who share your program's values, and the stronger you will repel those who do not share your ideals.

You are your group's most important recruiter.

Just by being the honest and authentic person you are, you are likely to attract people who share your same values. The more honest you are as a person, leader, and music organization, the more likely you are to attract people who will be successful in that environment.

If you are trying to "sell" your group by telling everyone how much fun it is, you will attract people who just want to have fun. While your intent may have been good, the result could be very bad. You may end up with a group of goofballs whose first priority is having a good time instead of getting better. You want to sell people on the good parts of the activity, but be careful not to sell something they are not ready to buy as you may regret it in the end. In music, we often times are so focused on attracting and recruiting new members, that we lose sight of what we are trying to repel. Before deciding on how to recruit, focus on who to recruit. Keep this saying in mind: "Music is good for everyone, but not everyone is good for music."

QUESTIONS

What are five attributes of the type of person you are trying to attract for your group?

____

____

____

On a daily basis, how often do you exhibit those same characteristics? (Circle one):

NEVER SOMETIMES OFTEN ALWAYS

List five attributes you are trying to avoid for your group:

____

____

____

In your group, do you focus your energy (time and attention) more on positive or negative behaviors?

List three negative behaviors that receive your time and attention:

List three positive behaviors that receive your time and attention:

List 10 things that you think could incentivize people to change their attitude (extra credit/ candy/praise/etc.):

1.
2.
3.
4.
5.
6.
7.
8.
9.
10.

"DON'T FIND THE FAULT,

FIND THE REMEDY."

— *Henry Ford*

12 PROBLEM PEOPLE

In this chapter, we will talk about how to deal with people in your group who are continually causing problems. They may not be "bad people"—just people doing "bad things."

Every leader will deal with conflict and turmoil at some point during their tenure as a leader. Why? Because conflict is an unavoidable byproduct of individuality. The fact that there are no two people on this planet that are exactly the same means that no two people will share exactly the same views on any given subject. That said, **it is not your difference of opinions, but how you respond to them that defines you as a leader**. Your success as a leader is not determined by your ability to agree, but your ability to disagree—and still move forward in a positive manner.

When dealing with "problem people," I find it best to remember that other than life and death, there are no absolutes in this world. Unfortunately, it is popular and often profitable to declare one's absolute "rightness." Our need to be right often overrides our ability to be objective. Once we have determined and decided upon our "rightness" we feel the need to share it with everyone around us.

Some people equate the size of one's audience to their level of expertise. Just because someone has a large following does not necessarily make them a great leader. Words matter and hold great power. So the greater following, the greater the responsibility to be aware of what you say and how you say it.

SOMEWHERE IN THE MIDDLE

When leading a group, even though you will face people who you believe to be difficult, that does not make them wrong and you right. Few ideas are as simple as black and white. Even black and white photos are mostly grey!

If we want music to be a place for everyone, then we have to be tolerant of people who might be very different from us. Keep in mind that as much as you may struggle with someone, they are struggling just as much with you.

It is a fair assumption that on the other side of the disagreement is someone who sees you as being *just as wrong as you see them*. The truth is probably somewhere in the middle, and your sentiments are based more on feelings than actual fact. People rarely fight over fact. It is our emotions *about* facts that impair our judgment during heated moments.

THE GREY AREAS OF DISCIPLINE

Conflict often comes as a result of discipline problems. Small issues (talking, being late, etc.) are escalated when not handled clearly and consistently. It's important for a leadership team to have a clear understanding of what the director's policy is on student discipline. For example, a group may need to answer questions like:

Are we allowed to/supposed to discipline other students?

What infractions should receive disciplinary measures, and what are those penalties?

What are we to do when something falls outside of the parameters of acceptable behavior?

In dealing with discipline, it's important to be proactive. Solve problems before they occur by having clear boundaries and consistent enforcement. Leaders who exhibit clarity, consistency and calmness, typically have much fewer problems that those who don't.

It's also worth examining whether you have rewards and incentives in addition to consequences and accountabilities. It not only "gamifies" the process and makes it more fun, but also shows that you are focusing time, effort, and resources on the students who are doing the right things.

But what about the ones who are doing the wrong things?

WHAT DEFINES GOOD DISCIPLINE POLICIES?

Discipline policies should be:

- Educational
- Non-punitive
- Productive
- Preventive

Next time someone is late to rehearsal, ask them to come in early the next day to set up for rehearsal. This creates a relationship between the offense and the response to it. It provides a teaching moment in a productive, non-aggressive way.

A FEW LAST THINGS TO REMEMBER ABOUT PROBLEM PEOPLE

- People are generally good and want to do the right thing.
- Most mistakes are made out of ignorance, not malice.
- People benefit when they're educated about the what, when, where, and why behind the rules.

QUESTIONS

List three or more incentives and rewards you have for students who make good choices:

____

____

____

List five more that you can think to add:

____

____

____

What are three rules that are most often violated in your group?

What proactive things can you do to specifically address these violations?

In your group or section, who are you most likely to struggle with this year?

List three things you can do to eliminate problems before they happen:

Does your age, personality, or lacking of musical or other skillsets put you in a position where problem people are more likely to take advantage of you in a leadership position?

What can you do to avoid this?

Are you willing to relinquish your power in order to maintain peace? If so, what powers could you give others to help them feel engaged and involved in the process?

Do you foresee problems with your friends who see you as their buddy and not their leader?

QUESTIONS

How might you be able to address these issues prior to them happening?

Do you use punishments as a leader (push ups/laps/etc.)?

If so, do you feel they are effective?

Share your worst "problem person" story in the space below. Please do not use names:

13 TYPICAL PROBLEMS

As a leader, every problem and situation is unique, not because of the problem itself, but because of the people and circumstances involved. While I don't believe that there are any universal answers to individual situations, experience tells us that there are some common problems that most groups face.

In this section, you will read about four typical problems, then answer a series of reflection questions to help you troubleshoot each one.

PROBLEM #1: TIME

This refers to tardiness or general absenteeism. This is the most prolific problem any large group faces. Typically, it is a small minority of people who commit the largest infractions. It can be assumed that your schedule is posted well in advance and is readily known, so people who are chronically absent/tardy are doing so not because of lack of information but due to a lack of personal accountability.

What is your group's attendance policy?

What are the consequences when people violate the policy?

Key Takeaway

It's important to know not only which battles are yours to fight, but also how to best fight them.

Do consequences escalate with each infraction? If not, why?

Who are the most likely offenders and what are some proactive steps you can take to address these issues before they become problematic?

PROBLEM #2: MUSICAL ACHIEVEMENT

The gap in musical skills and achievement in your ensemble are probably as vast as they are diverse. In the very same section, you might have an all-state player performing side-by-side with a beginner. Some groups may even have an eighteen-year-old with six years of experience playing alongside a thirteen-year-old with two years of experience.

Whatever the case may be, given the span of abilities and ages, it is impossible to believe that everyone will achieve at the same level and at the same rate.

Does your group have a "graduated" level of expectation for musical performance? If not, should you?

Key Takeaway

Take some time to step back and analyze the root/source of the problem so that you can best design the solution.

Is the grading curve or duration of time (memory checks/testing schedules) altered to provide more time to musicians who are younger or less experienced?

Does your group provide resources (lessons/sectionals) to help those who are struggling?

How important is musical mastery (playing) versus effort? Do you value one more than the other? What if someone is truly trying and practicing but is still struggling?

PROBLEM #3: ATTITUDE

Attitude is not something we are born with. It is something we learn from watching others. More than anything, it's a choice that is made.

Attitudes can be either systemic, localized, or individualized:

Systemic: Is the attitude pervasive throughout the ensemble and across multiple sections? If so, this likely comes from the ensemble environment and things outside of your control. In other words, it might be coming from adults, the community, or passed on from previous regimes and ensembles. If so, the only way to change a systemically bad attitude is to change systems. Rehearse differently, communicate differently, deal with discipline differently, etc. Big problems require big changes—mentally, emotionally, and physically.

Localized: Is the attitude confined to one group or section? If so, you need only deal with that section. It's best not to deal with the entire group when the damage is being done by a small group of individuals. Often times, but not always, this stems from the section leader. Deal with them first and the section next. Through it all, you have to show your support to those students who are choosing to behave in the correct manner.

Individualized: This is when just one or two apples are souring the entire bushel. Typically, this is where the best advice would be to try to see things from their perspective, to perhaps sit down and have a chat with them. But in my experience, this is a place for the director to get involved. Depending on the severity of the attitude problem, something may clearly be "out of whack" and is not likely to be fixed by a student leader. You can always give it a go yourself at first, but don't be afraid to ask your director for help if the problem isn't being resolved.

The other thing to consider when dealing with problematic attitudes—is that it might be you!

Yes, you!

It doesn't mean that you created the problem; it just means that your inherent differences may be making it harder for you as a leader to turn an attitude around.

What are some attitude adjustments you would like to make in your ensemble?

____

____

Are the attitudes systemic, localized, individualized, or a combination?

____

List three steps you could take to help resolve the issues:

____

____

____

What are the times and situations that conflict is most likely to occur?

____

____

Who might be better suited to deal with them and would they be willing and available to be a part of the solution?

____

____

Who might you be able to help and have influence that someone else is experiencing conflict with?

____

____

PROBLEM #4: THE GRIND

Let's be honest—the day-to-day of the season, contest prep, or any big goal your group works toward can start to feel like a demanding grind after awhile! The way we feel in August is not the way we feel in September or October. The way we feel when it's hot out is not the way we feel when it's cold out. The way we feel when we do something for the first time is not the way we feel when doing it for the hundredth time. This activity can and should be a grind. But a common challenge that groups face is feeling burned-out in the midst of it.

Luckily, there are a few ways that you can celebrate and embrace the grind. Talk about the grind openly and show people the progress they're making through it. Too often we wait until a performance or competition to chart growth. This delayed gratification is what leads to burnout and frustration. People don't mind working hard, but they want to see growth and get gratification from it, not just at the end of a season, but from month-to-month, week-to-week, day-to-day, and even hour-to-hour.

Think about it: Band camp, or the excitement about starting a season is not about a date on the calendar. People are excited because it's *something new*. People are excited because they see growth on the horizon, both in their group and in themselves. People are excited because they have new roles and responsibilities with new music. People want new. People want growth.

So how can we inject that same energy into the grind to break up some of the monotony? It's easier than you may think!

Key Takeaway

Even the best of groups have rough patches. Part of the word "persevere" is SEVERE! Through it all, remember that the good days and the bad days are just numbers on a calendar. What made them good or bad was the way we responded to them.

What are growth indicators (musical/visual/sectional/personal) that can be celebrated in the following intervals?

Daily: ______________________________

____

Weekly: ______________________________

____

Monthly: ______________________________

____

What are some metrics of growth that we can and should celebrate that we are not celebrating now?

____

____

____

What are some energizing games we played at the start that we could play again throughout the season?

What are some new activities/parties/games we can bring to the second and third month of the season?

Key Takeaway

As I like to say, band camp is not a date on a calendar, it's a state of mind. Change the mind, and you will change your group.

What are ways we can celebrate people who "embrace the grind?"

Find a quote about work ethic that inspires you and write it below. Tear it out of the book and tape it to your instrument locker or case so that you can be inspired each day.

Regardless of what you do, there will be a natural ebb and flow to the cycle and season, but if you acknowledge it, prepare for it, and respond to it in a celebratory way, you can minimize it's duration and impact.

UNIT 4
YOUR TOOLS

"I HAVE LEARNED OVER THE YEARS

THAT WHEN ONE'S MIND IS MADE UP,

THIS DIMINISHES FEAR;

KNOWING WHAT MUST BE DONE

DOES AWAY WITH FEAR."

—Rosa Parks

14 25 SELF-REFLECTION QUESTIONS

Use the following questions to start a meeting, end a meeting, or just as an interesting way to pass the time at a leadership retreat. They do not need to be done in any particular order and there are no right or wrong answers.

1. You heard a rumor from one person that someone is planning on bringing an inappropriate substance on a trip. The person is not a member of your section and is not someone you know very well. How would you handle the situation if the inappropriate substance was:
    a. Super Soaker squirt gun
    b. tobacco
    c. alcohol
2. You are in rehearsal and you hear someone from another section make a disparaging comment about his or her section leader under their breath. To be quite honest, you happen to agree with their comment. What do you do, if anything?
3. You are in the rehearsal room. Your director is not present, and a member of the senior class who is also the drum major shares with you their plan to "haze" freshman students at camp. There are rules at your school against hazing. What do you do?
4. You overhear a member of your section tell a member of the color guard that they are the reason your score was so bad at a recent competition. When you approach the member of your section, he points to the score sheets displayed in the director's window and states, "Do the math … it's true!" How do you respond?
5. You have a member of the band who is continually late to rehearsal. You have tried talking to him and it seems to do no good. You volunteered to pick him up, but that just makes both of you late, and you soon give up in frustration. What do you do now?
6. Should a senior be put in the top concert group just because they are graduating? What if they are very hardworking but are just not that talented? What if they play well enough, but there are already too many people in the top group who play that instrument?
7. Do you treat the members of your group equally when it comes to equipment? Do the freshmen get an equal shot at the best uniforms, instruments, lockers, sign-up sheets, etc.? If not, why? Is it justified?
8. How important is talent to your organization? How important is character? Which is more important?
9. You spot a fellow student from your group smoking off campus. Do you say something?

10. You attend a party on a Saturday night and you see members of the student leadership team drinking. Would you say or do anything? What if there were younger band members there? What if people were "trash-talking" their director at the party?
11. The night before an honor band audition, a member of your section tells you he is not going to show up to the audition he signed up for because he has not prepared for it. What would you say to him? Would you tell your director?
12. Have you ever broken a group rule and gotten away with it? What would have happened had you been caught?
13. Have you ever not given your best effort at rehearsal? If so, how can you justify speaking to your section about giving their best when they have seen you give less than your best?
14. Does your group behave the same in August as it does in November? If not, how does their behavior change? If their behavior gets worse over time, what can you do to combat that?
15. Does your staff play favorites? Is that acceptable? Should people who "do more" for the group get more benefits?
16. How are the leaders in your group chosen? Is this the best process? How would you improve it?
17. How does the rest of the campus perceive your group? Differentiate between how the band is perceived by the following groups: student council, the football team, cheerleaders, and the general student population. If the perception is not what you want it to be, what can you do to change that? Be specific to each group.
18. What parts of the group have the most staff support? Why? Do you think this is the best use of your resources?
19. What do you see as the greatest strengths of your ensemble? What do you see as the greatest weaknesses? How can you work towards minimizing the impact of your weaknesses?
20. Is there a favorite section in your group?
21. Is there a section that gets ignored?
22. Does the drum line or guard separate themselves from the group? What kinds of things could you put in place to combat that?
23. What is your favorite tradition? What would be a new tradition to start?
24. What are your teacher's best qualities?
25. How can you help your director be more efficient by taking on some tasks for him/her?

15 ACTIVITIES TO MAKE REHEARSALS MORE FUN

1. Have a "Christmas in July" party at band camp.
2. Organize a group of kids to play Christmas carols and go caroling one night. You can also carol to your administrators and the district office.
3. Submit a band announcement for the school marquee.
4. Visit a nursing home together.
5. Find a "pen pal" section in a band in another state or country, and start a message board with them.
6. Post instrument jokes about your instrument. You can find them on the internet. Read one every day at the start of rehearsal.
7. Run a sectional for the junior high band. Ask the director if he/she would like you to sit in for a rehearsal.
8. Send "friendship mail" to each member of your band before a performance. It can be anonymous or signed.
9. Challenge your staff to a game or contest.
10. Challenge another section to a game or contest.
11. Challenge another group on or off campus to a game or contest.
12. Have your sectional near a fountain or some other creative place.
13. Dress in costumes for your next rehearsal.
14. Bring a small grill and grill hot dogs on the field before a rehearsal.
15. Invite the local morning show to do a broadcast from your rehearsal.
16. Have a "dress like your director" day.
17. Make up a signature dance just for your group.
18. Have members exchange instruments for twenty minutes while learning drill.
19. Play for a local preschool.
20. Have a morning radio personality/DJ give a shout-out to your group.
21. Write to someone famous, asking them to write back to your section.
22. Put a "Slip 'N Slide" out during hot rehearsals and use it to cool off.
23. Have a drill down with the staff against students or staff against staff.
24. Do a skit for the whole band once a month.
25. Take a sectional picture in a goofy place and in a goofy way.

Your turn—add any ideas you have to this list!

"THE BEST WAY

TO PREDICT THE FUTURE

IS TO CREATE IT."

—*Abraham Lincoln*

16 WRITE A LETTER

In the space below, write a letter to yourself. The letter should be forward looking and talk about the challenges that lay ahead and the fears you have. The letter should be encouraging and speak to the goals you have as a leader and as a person. Think of it as your own personal pep talk.

When completed, turn the letter in to your director. Your letter will be returned to you at a special time and place.

Remember, the more you give to this letter, the more you will get!

"ALONE WE CAN DO SO LITTLE;

TOGETHER WE CAN DO SO MUCH"

— *Helen Keller*

17 LEADERSHIP PLEDGE

I recognize that I am human and that from time to time, I might fall short on expectations or my true potential. I also recognize that my fellow leaders and student musicians are equally flawed and will need my support, tolerance, and guidance throughout the year. Serving them is among my primary responsibilities as a leader. It is with this knowledge and understanding that I, as a member of the leadership team of this organization, pledge to do the following:

- Abide by all rules and regulations of this organization.
- Treat my peers and instructors with kindness and respect.
- When appropriate, assist in guiding others to do the same.
- Fully complete my assigned responsibilities and tasks in a timely and responsible manner.
- Try my best to always serve as a role model, both musically and personally.
- Put the needs of the group and it's members above those of my own.
- Support the director in the decisions he/she makes, even when I disagree.
- Support my fellow leaders in all of their endeavors and not place my needs above theirs.

In an effort to better myself and my group, I pledge to strive to do these things and more each and every day.

STUDENT SIGNATURE

DATE

"LEADERSHIP IS A CHOICE,

NOT A POSITION."

—*Stephen Covey*

18 LEADERSHIP REVIEW

As a leader, it is your job to provide assistance and performance feedback as needed. This chapter gives you the means to receive that same feedback from your section, fellow leaders, or director.

The following document is designed in two parts: self-reflection and outside feedback. You are to complete the self-reflection part on your own, submit that part to the reviewer (parent/teacher/fellow leader), and then they can add their notes and thoughts to yours.

Self-evaluation is hard.

You don't want to gloss over mistakes and flaws, but you also don't want to be overly critical. Do your best to strike the right balance between the two so that your fellow reviewer can give you the appropriate feedback and guidance to help you grow as a person and leader. This should be as much about celebrating what you are doing well as it is a chance to address areas where you are not as successful.

There is no way that anyone can honestly review you without you reviewing yourself first. It is the collaborative process that makes this meaningful.

If you are uncomfortable with putting your review in writing or having a formal evaluation, make it a point to stop by your director's office every couple of weeks for a "leadership review update."

These meetings can be as long or as short as necessary, giving you an opportunity to chat about the progress of your group and ways in which he/she could help you be more successful. If you feel like you are barely treading water, or worse, that you are drowning, then stop by sooner. If you feel like you are swimming along nicely, just stop by to say hi and exchange a quick touch-base.

Either way, this face-to-face time can also serve as an opportunity to share how you are doing with the balancing act between the demands of your group, your academic studies, and your "other life" pursuits. Yes, there is life outside of your music group (or at least there should be)!

Before answering the following questions, it may help you to jot down some notes and other thoughts on what is being asked in the questions. You might even want to interview some of your closest friends and family to get their perspectives. When done correctly, this is a worthwhile and meaningful assignment. Don't take the easy way out. Search your soul—it is where the best version of you lies.

NAME ______________________________

What are three things you are proud of as a leader?

Your answer: ______________________________

____

____

Reviewer's response: ______________________________

____

____

What are some things you think you could have handled better this year?

Your answer: ______________________________

____

____

Reviewer's response: ______________________________

____

____

Give yourself a grade as a leader and justify your answer:

Your Grade: ______

Justification: ______________________________

____

____

____

Reviewer's Grade: ______

Justification: ______________________________

____

____

____

What is one question you would like to ask about how to handle a particular problem moving forward?

Your question: ______________________________

____

Reviewer's response: ______________________________

____

____

What is an area of leadership strength that stands out for you?

Your answer: ______________________________

____

Reviewer's response: ______________________________

____

____

What is an area for leadership improvement that stands out for you?

Your answer: ______________________________

____

Reviewer's response: ______________________________

____

____

Share your final thoughts about this leadership journey:

____

____

____

Reviewer's response:

____

____

"A GENUINE LEADER

IS NOT A SEARCHER FOR CONSENSUS

BUT A MOLDER OF CONSENSUS."

—*Martin Luther King*

19 LEADERSHIP APPLICATION

The Student Leader Application is designed to:

1. Demonstrate commitment to the program.
2. Display student creativity.
3. Set a tone for the student leadership team.
4. Publicize and recruit for your program.
5. Serve as an educational activity, even if the student is not chosen for the position.

The successful completion of an application allows teachers to assess the various qualities of each applicant via their written words and actions. The combination of essay questions, service projects, and "Number 5" (described below, which is the most enjoyable part of the application) should give teachers a wealth of opportunities to display your knowledge, commitment, and creativity.

The essay component, which requires you to interview someone on campus regarding leadership views, will also lend credibility to the process and to your program. Teachers and administrators alike will have a new perspective on the program as they see the process and protocols used in selecting the leadership team. By interviewing fellow colleagues and administrators, you are acting as an ambassador for the program and should use this as an opportunity to advocate for your program.

The "Number 5," or as I like to call it, the "Dazzle Me," lets students do or create something that will display their passion and creativity. Some safeguards have been put in place (clean up your mess, no scavenger hunts, no time parameters) based on past experiences. Try to give students as much academic freedom with this as possible. With time, student projects will become more creative and grandiose, and application time will become an exciting process that students look forward to every year.

Perhaps the greatest benefit in this application is that it is WIN/WIN for the student and the sponsor. By merely applying, students are forced to examine themselves and assess who they are and what they believe. The program wins because it is the recipient of many service projects and creative activities that will energize and enthuse all the members of the program. In addition, the sponsor will receive a plethora of names to use as a recruiting database for the program.

LEADERSHIP APPLICATION

Welcome and thank you for showing an interest in being a part of the Student Leadership Team. *We hope you will find the application process to be interesting and enriching regardless of the outcome.* This application represents a significant departure from the standard way of selecting student leaders. In addition, some leadership positions have been added or removed to better fit the current organization. If you have any questions about the process or your application, please do not hesitate to contact your director at any time. Good luck, and work hard to best represent yourself through this process.

Your candidacy will be judged on the following criteria:

1. Past performance
2. Quality of your application
3. Future leadership potential
4. Best fit for the individual and organization

When completing the application, be thorough, creative, and honest. Don't say what you think your teacher/sponsor might want to hear. Say what you really think. Leaders are people who can offer something new and different to the organization. This application process is structured so that you will gain insights into yourself as a person, so please be honest and detailed. You need to open up and show the person who you truly are and what you aspire to be. Whether you are chosen to participate in the office you apply for is not the point. Dig deep inside, answer the questions, and complete the service project with the intent of learning something new. Please do not fill out this application unless you are prepared to participate in the leadership training process.

Positions available:	President	Vice-President
	Morale/Historian	Secretary/Librarian
	Drum Major	Section Leader
	Member at Large	Captain

All applications must be completed and all elements turned in by:____________________

Please be prompt and professional with your application. Some positions may need to participate in interviews and evaluations. You will be contacted to schedule an interview if this applies to you.

When submitting: Please make sure that all elements are enclosed in one package and are clearly labeled with your name. Any elements of your submission that you would like returned need to be labeled as such. All applications must be typed. Failure to do so will result in the return of the application to the applicant.

Rules for #5: HAVE FUN WITH THIS. There will be no class time given unless approval from

______________________________ is given prior to the event.

- No scavenger hunts.
- Do not set time restrictions on the director's time.
- Anything you do, you must be willing to undo upon request.

NAME ______________________________

POSITION(S) APPLYING FOR ______________ ______________

______________ ______________

______________ ______________

CURRENT G.P.A. ________ EMAIL ADDRESS ______________________

1. Please provide a resume. Be sure to highlight your past leadership roles and experiences.
2. On a separate piece of paper, please answer the following questions:

   What are your greatest personal strengths and how would the program benefit from them?

   What are some areas in which our organization could improve?

   What is something you are willing to commit to doing better as a member of the program?
3. Interview someone on your campus (student, faculty, or administrator) and ask him or her their views on leadership. What did you learn from your conversation? How were his/her views different from your own?

Complete the following projects:

4. Complete a service project for the organization. The scope and duration of the project are at your discretion. You may choose something that you think needs to be done, or you may ask the sponsor for a project. If you have any questions about the validity of your chosen project, please speak with the director prior to starting it.
5. Do something that dazzles us! This is where you have the opportunity to do something and show your creative side. You may do anything that you deem appropriate to convince us that you are able to "think outside the box" and show us your passion. This is the portion of the application where you should expect to invest the most time and show us something uniquely impressive about you. Therefore, take a risk here. Once again, this should be fun for you and the organization.

Please understand that if chosen, you will be held to a higher standard of behavior, performance, and work ethic than your peers. You must be willing to make that sacrifice so that others around you may succeed. Serving in this capacity will not only provide others with a better experience but will provide you with a tremendous growth opportunity that will serve you for years to come.

______________________ ______________________

STUDENT SIGNATURE PARENT SIGNATURE

Scott Lang

INSPIRING LEADERSHIP, LAUGHTER, and LEARNING

For over two decades, Scott Lang has been educating and entertaining audiences of all ages. As a nationally known leadership trainer, Scott conducts over 120 workshops annually and works with some of the country's finest educational groups and performing ensembles.

As a highly decorated teacher of sixteen years, Scott's bands have had many notable performances including: the Pasadena Tournament of Rose Parade, the Fiesta Bowl National Band Championship, the Music Educators National Biennial Conference, and for the President of the United States, William Jefferson Clinton.

Scott is a well-regarded author with over ten publications to his credit including: *Seriously?!*, *Leader of the Band*, *Leadership Success*, *Leadership Travel Guide*, *Leadership Survival Guide*, and is the creator of the highly successful Be Part of the Music series.

Mr. Lang currently resides in Chandler, Arizona with his beautiful wife, Leah, their sons, Brayden and Evan, and their highly irrational golden retriever, Rexie. He has breathed in and out approximately 264 million times and plans to keep on doing so until he doubles that number.

Alfred